The Sanda

WITHDRAWN

1 0 JUN 2022

The Sandal

A Story
by
TONY BRADMAN

Pictures by
PHILIPPE DUPASQUIER

Andersen Press · London

Yesterday, 77 B.C.

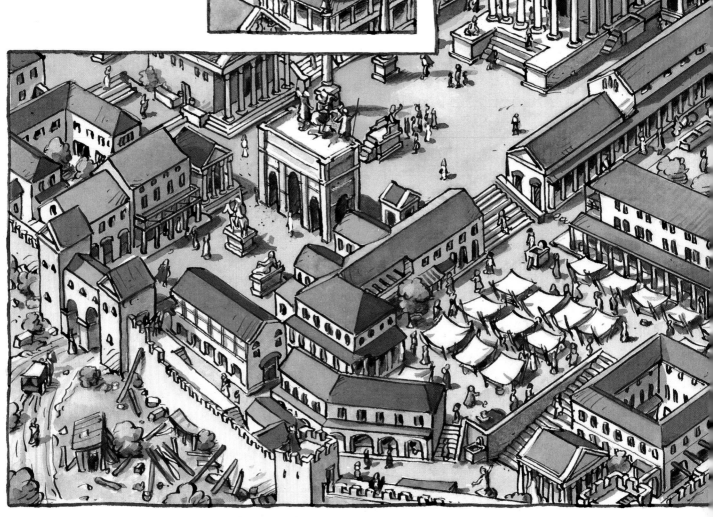

Today

"Where is that sandal?"

Dad looked cross. My little sister is always losing things, especially her shoes. And she always loses them at just the wrong moment, like when Dad is getting us ready to go out.

Dad found the sandal at last.

"Come on, you two. We'll never get there at this rate."

We went to the park first. It was great.

My little sister enjoyed herself so much she didn't want to leave.

But she soon came when Dad and I walked to the gate.

"Where are we going now, Dad?" I asked.

"To one of my favourite places," he said.

It was a museum. As soon as we went in, I decided I liked it too.

I liked the interesting things in glass cases. I liked the statues and the pictures, and all the little models and maps.

My little sister liked the stairs... and the open spaces... and the things she could climb on.

"Don't do that!" said Dad. "I think it's time we went home."

On our way out, my little sister stopped suddenly. "Sandal!" she said. There in a case was a sandal, exactly like one of my little sister's. But it was old...very, very old. It was a Roman sandal.

"It's just your size," said Dad.

Dad and my little sister walked on. I looked at the sandal, and thought of that other little girl, all those years ago...I wonder if she had a brother, too?

"Come on, slowcoach!" called Dad.

We left the museum and crossed the road. We stopped on the bridge to look at the swirling water below.

"Sandal!" said my little sister. We looked down . . . and saw one of her sandals fall into the river.

There was a tiny splash, and it was swept away. I saw it bobbing on the water for a while . . . and then it was gone.

Dad was cross, but my little sister was too tired to be told off. In fact . . . she had fallen asleep.

"Ah well," said Dad, "maybe someone will find the sandal one day."

Maybe someone will, I thought. Maybe someone will . . .

Tomorrow, 2250 A.D.

More Andersen Press paperback picture books!

MICHAEL
by Tony Bradman and Tony Ross

A COUNTRY FAR AWAY
by Nigel Gray and Philippe Dupasquier

THE PICNIC
by Ruth Brown

OUR PUPPY'S HOLIDAY
by Ruth Brown

I'LL TAKE YOU TO MRS COLE
by Nigel Gray and Michael Foreman

THE MONSTER AND THE TEDDY BEAR
by David McKee

THE HILL AND THE ROCK
by David McKee

FROG IS A HERO
by Max Velthuijs

THE LONG BLUE BLAZER
by Jeanne Willis and Susan Varley

First published in Great Britain in 1989 by Andersen Press Ltd., 20 Vauxhall Bridge Road,
London SW1V 2SA. This paperback edition first published in 2000 by Andersen Press Ltd.
Published in Australia by Random House Australia Pty., 20 Alfred Street, Milsons Point,
Sydney, NSW 2061. All rights reserved.
Colour separated in Switzerland by Photolitho AG, Gossau, Zürich.
Printed and bound in Italy by Grafiche AZ, Verona.

10   9   8   7   6   5   4   3   2   1

British Library Cataloguing in Publication Data available.

ISBN 0 86264 843 2

This book has been printed on acid-free paper